For David

Copyright © 1996 by Colin West

All rights reserved.

First U.S. edition 1996

Library of Congress Cataloging-in-Publication Data

West, Colin.
"I don't care!" said the bear / Colin West.—1st U.S. ed.
Summary: The big brown bear has no fear of a bad-tempered goose, a big pig,
or even a wolf, but something very small causes him to run scared.
ISBN 1-56402-807-0
[1. Bears—Fiction. 2. Mice—Fiction.
3. Fear—Fiction. 4. Stories in rhyme.] I. Title.
PZ8.3.W4997Iag   1996
[E]—dc20   95-35203

10 9 8 7 6 5 4 3 2 1

Printed in Hong Kong

This book was typeset in Plantin Semibold.
The pictures were done in pen and ink and watercolor.

Candlewick Press
2067 Massachusetts Avenue
Cambridge, Massachusetts 02140

"I DON'T CARE!" SAID THE BEAR

COLIN WEST

CANDLEWICK PRESS
CAMBRIDGE, MASSACHUSETTS

"There's a moose on the loose!"
said the teeny-weeny mouse.

"I don't care," said the bear,
with his nose in the air.

"There's a moose on the loose
and a bad-tempered goose!"
said the teeny-weeny mouse.

"I don't care," said the bear,
with his nose in the air.

"There's a moose on the loose
and a bad-tempered goose
and a pig who is big!"
said the teeny-weeny mouse.

"I don't care," said the bear,
with his nose in the air.

"There's a moose on the loose
and a bad-tempered goose
and a pig who is big
and a snake from a lake!"
said the teeny-weeny mouse.

"I don't care," said the bear,
with his nose in the air.

"There's a moose on the loose
and a bad-tempered goose
and a pig who is big
and a snake from a lake
and a wolf from the north!"
said the teeny-weeny mouse.

"I don't care!" said the bear,
with his nose in the air.

"There's a moose on the loose
    and a bad-tempered goose
    and a pig who is big
    and a snake from a lake
    and a wolf from the north
    and a teeny-weeny mouse!"
    said the teeny-weeny mouse.

"YIKES!" said the bear.
And he leaped in the air!

Then that great big
old bear ran off
back to his lair.

3